TAKE ME

A Paranormal Monster Romance

V. P. Nightshade

Sohmer Publishing

CONTENTS

COPYRIGHT

Take Me

EPUB ISBN: 978-1-960139-24-5

Paperback ISBN: 978-1-960139-25-2

First edition

A BIG THANK YOU!

To My Readers ~
*Who are looking for something short
with a little more bite~
I look forward to reading
your reviews and comments!*

To My Sons ~
*Always work hard,
and good things will come to you!*

As always, to that Grumpy Man ~
I'm glad you are still paying my bills!
I love you, baby!

TAKE ME

A **DARK**, **ADDICTIVE MONSTER** romance from author **V. P. Nightshade.**

For fans of obsession, erotic horror, and fated mates that burn the world down.

By day, Lina Vex disappears.

By night, she dances for the dark.

At Nocturne Lounge, she's the girl in white—mysterious, untouchable, hypnotic. But behind the blank eyes is a woman unraveling. The dreams have started. The sigils on her skin glow. And the man watching her from the shadows?

He isn't human.

Ezren Marr is an Incubane—an ancient creature who feeds not on blood, but on surrender. He takes only what his prey gives in the heat of passion. But Lina? She's different. She doesn't resist. She *offers*. And that terrifies him.

What begins as erotic obsession becomes something sacred. Dangerous. Transformative.

Because Lina isn't just prey. She's becoming something else.

When she begs to be taken, Ezren doesn't just feed.

He falls.

And she rises.

Take Me is a standalone, 20,000-word paranormal romance featuring monster worship, dreamlike seduction, and supernatural heat.

No cliffhanger
No cheating
Just darkness, devotion, and one hell of a bite.

CONTENT & TRIGGER WARNINGS

TAKE ME IS A dark, monster romance that contains psychological horror elements and intense themes and mature content. It may not be suitable for all readers.

This story includes:

- **Suggestive Content/Sexual Themes**, including public performance, mirror play, and supernatural orgasm

- **Monster/human dynamics** (non-human anatomy, psychic seduction)

- **Dream sequences** that blur fantasy and reality

- **Power exchange, worship kink, and sacred surrender**

- **Supernatural obsession and possessive desire**

- **Bloodplay** (non-violent, consensual, self-inflicted)

- **Emotional trauma, dissociation, and erotic grief**

- **Depictions of psychological unraveling**

- **Dark sensual imagery and intense emotional dependency**

This is a work of **fictional, consensual fantasy** involving adult characters. While themes of control, surrender, and supernatural domination are explored, *Take Me* is grounded in **mutual desire, agency, and fated connection**.

Reader discretion is advised.

EPIGRAPH

She Took Me

She danced like blasphemy wrapped in lace,
A sacrament smeared across time and space.
Not prey, not gift, but a god in disguise—
With hunger like thorns and heaven in her thighs.

I watched from the dark with a mouth full of need,
Built to devour, to drink, to feed.
But she came to the altar with fire in her breath—
And carved her name in the walls of my death.

I did not take her.
She took me.

Broke me in half with a whisper, a kiss.
Fed me surrender, called it abyss.
Her hands on my throat were a holy decree—
"You're mine now," she said, and I ceased to be.

My wings have wilted, my sigils gone cold,
The hunger I was now begging to hold.

She left me a ruin, divine and undone—
A monster unmade by the touch of *one*.

So let them call her cursed or mad—
She gave me the only soul I had.
And if I burn, I'll burn with glee—
Because she didn't fall.

She rose.
And took me.

~V. P. Nightshade
Read by the Author
   https://youtu.be/NIAOq3szQYw

PAINTED IN WHITE

THE BASS HIT LOW, dirty, and deep—like the city's heartbeat bleeding through the cracked foundation of the Nocturne Lounge. Smoke curled under strobes. Bodies moved, hypnotized, sweaty, feral in the thick air.

Lina Vex took the stage like a woman made of mist and silk. Dressed in white—a gauzy slip that clung to her hips and hung off one shoulder. No bra, no shoes. Her long blonde hair, like molten sunshine, spilled down her back in waves, damp at the ends. Her skin, pale with a hint of gold beneath the lights, seemed to shimmer with each movement. Her mouth was painted the same deep red as her nails.

Her eyes—storm-cloud gray, rimmed in kohl—swept across the room without truly seeing anyone.

Blank. Hollow. Beautiful.

She didn't smile. She didn't wave. She didn't flirt with the front row.

She simply existed—otherworldly, as if she stepped out of a fever dream painted in smoke and sorrow.

The spotlight followed her curves like a lover's hand. Her body moved in slow, sinuous arcs—each step a whisper, each motion sharpened with aching restraint. She didn't dance for them. Not the wolves in pressed collars, not the drunk girls pressed against the rail.

She danced for the dark.

At the far corner of the lounge, cloaked in half-light, sat Ezren Marr; a man no one knew. Always the same booth. Always untouched liquor on the table before him.

No one remembered how they knew his name. No one remembered when he'd first appeared.

But Lina saw him; saw him like she did every night.

Tonight, his eyes burned brighter. Black ringed with red. Still. Watching.

Behind the bar, Mick Carroway, owner of the Nocturne Lounge, polished a glass with a rag stained from years of use. He squinted toward the stage. "You ever seen her blink?"

Cassie Palomo—Red to everyone but Lina—leaned against the counter in her red wig, black crop top, barely-there leather miniskirt, and combat boots. She flicked her cigarette into the ashtray without missing a beat. "Only when she's about to break."

Mick snorted. "She'll shatter one of these nights, Red."

Cassie's gaze flicked to the shadowed booth. "Or someone's gonna do it for her."

On stage, Lina turned her back to the crowd. Arms outstretched, head tilted toward the ceiling like she was offering herself to something unseen. And maybe, just maybe, she was.

***

Later, she walked home barefoot.

The boots she'd worn had vanished. Her purse too. She didn't remember the walk from the club, only the press of cool concrete beneath her soles and the sound of her own blood roaring like music in her ears.

Somewhere between the back alley of the Lounge and the rusted gate of her apartment building, time folded. She remembered the sensation of walls pulsing around her, a door opening that shouldn't exist, wind whispering her name.

The streetlights flickered.

Her skin had felt too hot, her breath too slow.

And then—

A wall. Brick. Damp. Rough against her spine.

Breath warmed her neck, a deep exhale that wasn't hers. Hands—one at her hip, the other cradling the side of her throat.

Not choking.

Claiming.

His body pressed into hers, solid and cold as stone and yet somehow burning. His leg slid between hers, parting her thighs until she gasped. Her back arched. She moaned into the night air before she could stop herself.

No one was there.

But he was. He had to be.

Looking back towards the wall she was pinned against, she could still see the outline of his body, his muscular arms and determined expression, the way his lips parted with an unspoken desire.

The shadows danced around them, shifting and contorting like liquid ink.

His lips never touched her skin—but she felt the shape of his mouth at her pulse point, open, hungry. The air around them thickened, buzzed, filled with something old and electric. His fingers flexed on her hip, and she swore a painful light flared to life in response—burning beneath her skin like a buried star.

Her body bowed. Her panties dampened. Her knees went weak, but he held her there—suspended between brick and breath and something much deeper. Desire flooded her like heat down her spine; low, and hard, and thick.

Then—nothing.

The air emptied. The streetlights buzzed back to normal.

She stood there alone, trembling.

Maybe it had been a dream.

But her thighs were still slick. Her lips still tingled. Her core still clenched around the echo of a presence she couldn't name.

No one saw her. No one stopped her.

Maybe she'd imagined the way the shadows reached for her legs like oil.

***

Inside her tiny apartment, she stripped off the white dress and dropped it on the floor. The bathroom mirror flickered under the flickering bulb—halos of light blooming and dying like breaths.

The air was still and heavy with the lingering scent of desire, the sweet and heady aroma of sweat and arousal filling the small space.

Her skin steamed with perspiration. Her lips were swollen. Her nipples ached as though someone had sucked them too hard.

Lina stepped closer.

A faint symbol glowed on the inside of her left hip. Circular. Sigil-like. Not a tattoo. Not something she remembered. When she blinked, it faded. When she gasped, it flared again.

She raised her fingers to her lips. They trembled.

The dream. The faceless man. The command whispered like a sin: *Let go.*

She'd obeyed.

And somewhere deep inside, in a place her mind couldn't touch, she knew he'd been real.

***

She didn't go to the Lounge that night.

She sat in her apartment with the lights off and the blinds drawn, as if she could shut the world out by pretending she didn't want it. Her gauzy white dress lay in a crumpled heap near the bathroom door like the ghost of the woman who'd worn it. She told herself she needed rest, that her body ached from dancing, that nothing had happened in the alley but a flash of drunk fantasy and sleep deprivation.

But her body said otherwise.

Her body was a symphony of sensations, each note pulsing with a fervent desire that she couldn't deny. It sang to her in a language of aching and longing, aching for the touch of another and longing for the release of her inhibitions. Despite her attempts to rationalize and dismiss her feelings, her body reveled in the undeniable truth that she had been touched, owned, and claimed in ways that words could never express.

She hadn't let herself fall asleep. She'd stayed up until almost dawn, legs folded beneath her, spine against the wall, the mattress a thousand miles away. With a black ink pen, she drew a latticework of small x's and o's up and down her thighs and over her knees.

Tic-tac-toe games no one would ever win.

Every time the furnace exhaled through the vent, she flinched.

She told herself it wasn't real.

She told herself that again when she finally collapsed into bed, the ink still tacky and her heart still racing. But her body betrayed her the moment she closed her eyes.

***

She woke with the taste of his mouth still lingering on her tongue—salt and smoke, like iron pressed between her teeth. Half choke, half moan, the sound escaped her lips as she twisted in the sheets—pulse fluttering beneath her ribs like a trapped moth.

His voice echoed like dark velvet against the raw walls of her mind.

Lina. Let go.

She bolted upright, drenched in sweat, heart hammering. The sheets stuck to her chest, her stomach, her thighs. The heat between her legs was unbearable.

She pressed her hand to the swell of her hip, where the faint shimmer of the sigil still burned beneath the skin.

Real. Circular. Hungry.

Her breath caught. She pulled the sheet back and stared.

There were bruises—finger-width shadows on her hipbones, a single thumbprint high on her inner thigh. Her skin tingled beneath her own touch.

The dream hadn't faded. It clung to her skin like smoke, coiled in the sheets, whispered from the walls. She could still feel his weight pressing her down. His mouth hovering over her pulse. The slow, relentless drag of unseen fingers along her inner thigh.

And the hunger.

God, the hunger.

She hadn't been touched like that in years—if ever. She had let no one hold her that way.

But him?

She hadn't just let him.

She'd begged.

The walls of the apartment pulsed. The mirror across the room flickered. She wrapped her arms around her knees and rocked, slow and silent, a tremble in her breath that wouldn't stop.

It wasn't real.

It couldn't have been real.

She stumbled to the bathroom and turned on the shower. The spray hit her skin cold and sharp, then shifted into thick steam that blurred her reflection until she couldn't tell where her body ended and the mirror began.

But the sigil stayed.

So did the bruises.

And when she stepped back from the glass, she saw it again—her reflection lingering a heartbeat too long, eyes too knowing, mouth parted like she'd just whispered *yes*.

Eyes wide. Lips parted. Skin glowing.

She didn't know who that girl was.

Another sigil flared faintly beneath her navel, warm as a mouth against her skin.

She dried off and dressed in silence. No makeup. No music. Just the sound of the radiator ticking and her heart cracking open in slow, measured beats.

She stared at her reflection for an hour.

Then she picked up her bag, opened the door, and walked into the dark.

***

At the Nocturne, the smoke and sweat wrapped around her bare limbs and the thick pulse of music vibrated like heartbeats beneath her feet.

He was there, eyes on her from the same shadowed corner.

Like always.

He could make it real.

She only had to let go.

She wanted to.

Oh, god, she wanted to.

THE MAN IN THE SHADOWS

LINA FOUND HER FOOTING on the stage, unsure whether she danced or surrendered as the air itself pulsed and flickered with tension, a net of shadows catching her bare skin and holding her, suspended and unraveling. The slip that clung to her sweat-dampened frame was both vestment and vice; the strobe lights flared across her body in waves, beatific and feral, making her moves raw and primal, like possession or exorcism.

She locked eyes with Ezren, and the rest of the club disappeared into silence, the dense atmosphere threading itself through her veins until each sway and arc of her limbs sent a lightning charge of desire to her core. Her body betrayed her, aroused, and exposed, and insatiable. She moved in a trance: oblivion and release crashing through her like tidal waves.

The world bent and blurred as she spun through it, the music surging from dim to deafening in erratic strokes of sensation, consuming each thought, leaving only him. She lost herself, and then lost herself again, collapsing and catching, like the whole stage dropped away beneath her. At the corners of the room, the shadows moved as though they breathed, holding their own slow rhythm. Lina wound through their thick embrace until everything felt drenched in night.

She couldn't tell if she followed the beat, or it followed her; if the desperate ache building in her was real or imagined. The feeling overtook her—an undertow, an invitation—and the harder she tried to surface, the deeper it drew her under. Her skin seemed to dissolve into the heat and the movement, each sharp breath tasting like metal and thunder. She wondered what he would do if she stopped, if she dropped right there at his feet, panting and half-conscious with want ... need ... or if that was what he intended.

Ezren's eyes smoldered like molten coals, their black depths encircled by crimson rings that burned like embers. His towering frame was a study in contrasts—lean yet powerful, moving with an otherworldly grace that seemed to defy the shadows around him. Pale skin shimmered with a silver-oil sheen, appearing impossibly cold except for when passion ignited it. Long, black hair cascaded down his back like liquid midnight, and as she blinked, it looked to be framing crown-like obsidian antlers etched with glowing sigils.

As he melted into the darkness, the only thing she could still see was the intensity of his eyes, and Lina unraveled into pure desire.

The crowd vanished. Only their gaze remained, spanning the shadows, locked on each other. Her body reeled beneath the force of it, snapped, and swayed, and sang.

Her silk slip clung to her as if afraid of drowning, tracing each line of her trembling figure, each flash of vulnerability. She might have been both captive and deity, crucified on Ezren's silent insistence, stripped of every last control. Sweat stung her eyes, but she never dared break their electric connection to blink it away. Her breath shivered in her chest, but she kept moving, bare feet catching on the rough wooden stage, legs spreading wide and wild to brace herself against a release she didn't even understand. She looked beatific, unhinged, collapsing beneath the magnitude of his hunger.

She looked undone.

Lina's blood seemed to boil, and her insides coiled tighter, tighter, ready to snap. The light flared. Her mind went dark, and Ezren's gaze engulfed her.

Then everything stopped.

***

"Lina!" Cassie's voice broke the frantic rhythm, and her hand caught Lina's shoulder as she turned, reeling, behind the stage. "You alright? You look like you're miles away."

Lina nodded, silent. Her eyes never left the darkened booth as the bass kicked back into being, blurring around her like static. The air felt colder, thinner. She wondered if anyone saw her quiver. She wondered what Ezren saw.

Cassie watched Lina with suspicion sharp as her eye makeup, leaning one shoulder against the crumbling brick wall. She flicked the dancer's cheek with one long black fingernail. "Earth to Lina? You want to say anything to let me know you're alive, or just keep staring like a—"

"I'm fine." Her voice was a soft echo of itself. Lina shifted beneath the weight of Cassie's scrutiny, felt the dark circles and pale lips like new bruises. "Just—fine."

"That wasn't the word I was going to use." Cassie narrowed her eyes. "But you do you."

Lina nodded again, more to herself than Cassie, her damp hair sticking to the back of her neck. The last threads of their conversation caught and tangled as she moved away from Cassie's silhouette into the shadow-soaked backstage. Her heart pounded too fast, almost painful, though she wasn't sure if it was from fear or exhilaration. Her body ached and sparkled, demanding to feel Ezren's stare scorch it anew, willing her to double back, to crawl to him like some sleek, breathless animal and collapse into oblivion.

The wooden slats beneath her feet were rough, but they felt intimate and soft, like she stepped through water instead of the dim, humid air. Her pulse rattled the bones of the club itself, straining to escape the confines of her ribs. She brushed a shaking hand across her flushed face and smiled faintly, madly. As though something already knew, a bright shiver blazed beneath the skin on her hip and her chest, and it hurt with need.

The mirrored dressing room pulled at her, an irresistibly dangerous promise, and her breath caught sharp in her throat. This was what it felt like to drown.

It wasn't possible. Nobody else had been here.

Lina froze at the open doorway, barely seeing the mottled and streaked glass of the antiquated mirrors, barely noticing the spindly shadows of backstage reflected, twisting into the open mouths of demons. Her eyes focused only on the steamed surface and the words it bore. The lights crackled and dimmed above her, and the room felt vast, expanding. Her breath hitched and disappeared in the thickening air.

COME.

The letters dripped their commanding message, cool and silver, and seemed to beat with their own knowing insistence, like each was an extension of the fevered sigil beneath her clothes, beneath her skin.

She took a ragged step closer, holding her breath until it flared again like a furnace, heating her mouth and her chest. Until it took her, and she couldn't see or feel or imagine anything else.

Lina's fingers hovered over the writing, pale and trembling against the fogged glass. For a breathless instant, she thought about staying, about abandoning the heaviness and horror and every part of her not already lost. For a breathless instant, she thought about being unafraid, unanchored, everything she would never be.

Her touch on the glass felt hot, and slick, and alive. She couldn't tell whether the warmth came from the air or from herself, whether the fogged glass shivered at her presence or whether it was the other way around. She didn't care. She let the heat pull her deeper, drank the invitation with closed eyes, absorbed the word's silken promise through every pore until it remade her in its own untethered image. Until the world shrank to nothing but herself and Ezren's absence.

Until her lungs burned like lit fuses, and she pulled back, just enough to want him more.

The mirrors spun as she backed away, resolving into images and fractures of herself that dripped like candle wax, dissolving with the condensation. She could see how red her mouth looked, how gold the circles under her eyes burned, how wide and empty they had grown.

As she stumbled from the room, she caught her reflection in the discolored corners, smaller and smaller, more ghost than girl.

The rest of the club broke over her like a waking dream, but Lina moved through it, still asleep, suspended between everything she craved and everything she couldn't bring herself to touch. The bodies in the darkness twisted and swayed with their own pale, submerged beauty, though none held a candle to his.

Not anymore. Maybe not ever.

Her mind blurred the shadows into Ezren's shape, and her legs followed.

His silence echoed, and she heard it more clearly than the bass or the half-muffled shouts. It turned the smallest touch of sweat on her flushed skin into a molten reminder. It let her believe, for a desperate instant, that she'd find him just by looking. It made her lose herself again, drowning in what she couldn't have.

The air was impossibly thick and unbearably sweet as it gathered around her and followed into the city streets, as the corners of her mouth pulled into a small, mad smile.

It let her think, for a moment longer, that she had never left the club at all.

And the hunger roared.

She wondered what would be left when this hunger passed. Would she still be her, or would she be someone else?

Maybe she was already someone else.

***

The door to the street swung open and pulled her outside, into a night that bled color and sound, into the world she thought she'd left behind. Lina was lost to it. Her skin was flushed with the imprint of every stolen breath. Her mind sparked with thought and memory until she couldn't tell one from the other, until she couldn't tell if she even cared.

It wasn't far. That's what she told herself. Just enough to get the gnawing ache out of her lungs, out of her legs. It would only take a minute.

It would take forever.

She hesitated beneath the sickly amber streetlights, waiting for the rush of city life to fill the space that stretched between her bones, the new and gnawing emptiness she didn't recognize. She hadn't noticed how far she ran, how frantically the hunger moved her. She was a block or two from the river, maybe less, maybe more. She didn't care. She leaned into the cold as it tightened around her, pressing her sharper ... truer. She pretended the chill was enough to keep her there, not the frenzy of his absence, not the molten demand, the ragged heat it left her with.

As she slowed, the air crackled like parchment and drifted behind her, desperate, and delicate, and burning. The sigils flared gold beneath her skin, not gentle but furious. They flashed above the streetlamps, flickered like breaking bulbs. Her bare feet slapped and stung the pavement. The throbbing rhythm filled her, the frantic rhythm of her heart. She couldn't slow it, couldn't outpace it. She gave up and ran.

Lina's body moved faster than the thoughts she used to know, and every block unraveled her further. Desire pricked the insides of her thighs, tugged her toward something weightless, reckless. She pulled the night deeper into her, let it twist and swell like a lungful of dark.

The deeper she drank, the faster it grew.

***

She wasn't sure if she found the club or if it found her. The shadows curled and whispered like they'd never lost track of her, and the way she drifted up the alley and into their thick embrace made her wonder. They closed around her and stole the dampness of her breath. They bled into the thin white of her slip. She thought she heard a voice behind her, then another, growing louder, doubling back, more than a voice, and she didn't stop.

The glow of the city pulled back as the club pulled her in, a candle-lit night sky folding around a wayward star.

It was darker and heavier, each molecule swollen with arousal and defeat. She was out of herself and beyond herself, cast so far adrift that her body hardly felt her own. As she moved through the club, it hummed with familiar unreality.

She wondered whether this was what ghosts felt like, if they felt like anything. She thought about the otherworldly, about less, about too much, and couldn't tell them apart. She almost wanted to turn back, to get out of the dizzying air that rippled over her, that licked at her, and find a place where her breath was steady.

She almost wanted to stay. Wanting one or the other; terrified of both.

A silhouette broke through the swirling bodies.

"Didn't think I'd see you again." Mick's voice took form as she got closer, as she edged toward the bar, toward the hall that split open at the club's back like an invitation, toward the stairwell leading toward the second floor; like it was a command she had to obey. "Least of all tonight."

His attention was pointed but didn't need to be. He never looked at anything he didn't already know the truth about.

Her eyes, gold-rimmed and cloud-split, flicked over him, never settling on the grizzled edges. "It's not what you think."

She wondered if it was true.

He dried a glass that didn't need it, the pale streak of his arm moving like an apparition across the hazy barroom. "You don't even know what I think, kid."

He was right, and she hated it, hated him, hated everything but the need and the sharp relief as she gave herself to it.

She turned, leaving her response and everything else unfinished.

She heard him shout behind her, the tone gentler than the words. "Are you sure that's where you want to go? Nobody's been on that floor in years!"

Lina let herself forget the words as she passed the mirrors lining the club's walls. Her reflection flashed between moments of deep, tremulous shadow. Her movements blurred, fractured. She thought of herself with less and less certainty. When the thin light and the heavy dark broke across her face, her body, they looked molten and fluid and like she never wanted them to stop.

They didn't. The deep dark followed her into the hall, wrapped her up in it like a too-tender goodbye. Her body flushed red against it, impossibly warm and impossibly cold, gone, almost beyond feeling.

Gone, almost, to anything but need.

Her reflection broke over the bruised walls, her own face staring from uneven patches of mirrored glass. She watched it come undone.

Her bare feet brushed against specks of dust that tickled her nostrils. She breathed them in, swallowed the strangeness. The air was a living thing, with and without form, a creature inside her chest. Her mouth felt full of stars and ink as if she had swallowed the cosmos.

She didn't stop.

The word from the mirror burned beneath her skin, its silken promise racing like a fever through her veins. The walls stretched in dark surrender, shrank in trembling impatience. They dripped candlelight and thick shadow. They collapsed around her, miles closer than they should have been. The corridor shivered, the line between danger and deliverance a flicker beneath her bare, burning soles.

It wavered with each step she stepped.

The black door was only the beginning.

It stood open in invitation, and Lina pushed the rest of the way inside, her mind dark and expectant and like it had always known. The room felt like forgetting. It smelled of wax and wine and gave everything back in ghostly drops and dim flashes.

The only light came from candles, melting and guttering, their reflections tall and bright on the mirrors' opaque glass. They moved as if to breathe was to blur. Her breath was a strange and fluid thing, a disembodied and radiant thing. It pulled away with the damp heat and spun.

He stood there, shirtless, pale and unwavering. A striking figure bathed in the flickering candlelight; reflected over and over in the mirrored walls. His bare chest was a canvas of pale skin and hard cut muscle, shimmering with a silvery sheen that seemed to drink in the shadows around him. The obsidian antlers atop his head arched gracefully, like a regal crown, their surfaces etched with glowing sigils that pulsed softly in the dim light. Cascading down his shoulders, his long silky black hair moved with a fluid grace reminiscent of dark water, framing a face both haunting and mesmerizing. From his back unfurled leathery black wings, their edges sharp and sleek as they stretched outward, casting intricate patterns across the mirrored walls. Each movement was deliberate and predatory, exuding an unearthly allure that was impossible to ignore.

His body spoke of desire and undoing, and glimmered like water caught between liquid and ice.

Ezren stepped forward.

Slow. Soundless. His movement was fluid, unnatural—like light bending through water. The shadows clung to him as though reluctant to release their claim. He crossed the room with a grace that didn't belong to this world until he stood just inches in front of her.

He raised one hand, fingers extended—not touching. They hovered just above her jaw, then dipped lower to her throat, lower still to the base of her sternum, where another sigil pulsed beneath her skin. She swore the candle flames leaned toward her, drawn by the electricity between them, and his breath chilled the space where it met hers.

Her body pulsed with awareness. Her lips parted on a gasp. Her knees weakened beneath her, but she didn't fall.

He still hadn't touched her. But he didn't need to.

She felt him inside her head—not as a voice, but as sensation. Like his hunger had found its way into her bloodstream, warmed her spine, and took root in the hollow beneath her ribs.

His eyes stripped her where she stood. And it was a gift. A hunger that wanted her whole, not hollowed.

She opened to it.

Her breathing licked around them and pressed tighter. She caught it in small gulps, like it was his and not hers.

He took nothing. He took everything.

Ezren's eyes burned, red and violent, in the flickering air. He looked more unearthly than ever, more beautiful, more monstrous, more ready to be split by the single word he didn't have to say.

Her body throbbed with the distance and pulled her in. Her mind went light and empty and fell.

Lina didn't know whether to brace herself against his desire or allow herself to be completely dismantled by it. She braced herself anyway, pressing into the dark frame of the door, her lungs shallow, insistent.

Her hips lifted.

The light.

She unfolded like his wings, like heaven.

His presence eclipsed hers, and she folded. She filled.

Her skin flashed with the brightness of an exploding sun. The air expanded to meet it, slick and white hot.

She shook with everything she was and everything she wanted, with more than release and less than surrender. The building heat went tight and breathless, tighter, more breathless, until all she had left was molten gold, blazing desire, Ezren, and need.

"Let me see what's mine."

His voice slipped into her like a second climax—soft, commanding, and absolutely certain.

Her body broke on it. Opened on it.

His eyes closed, lips parted—not in hunger, but in awe.

"Yes," he breathed.

And she shattered.

***

Her own bare feet carried her into the street, dazed and glistening.

The outside world took hold, a dull ache. It pulsed with each stolen step.

It pulsed with every heartbeat.

THE MIRROR GAME

LINA HADN'T MEANT TO return.

She'd told herself she wouldn't. That once was enough. That she could survive the ache. That she could hold her breath long enough to surface.

But desire didn't ask for permission.

It pulled her like a tide, low, and dark, and endless, and by the time she reached the base of the stairwell, her feet were already bare. Her skin already burning. Her pulse already dancing to a rhythm only he could summon.

This was not the first time she had climbed the stairs above the Nocturne Lounge.

But this time, she knew what waited.

And still she went.

The air thickened around her like velvet soaked in breath and ruin. The stairwell had changed—or maybe she had. It felt longer now, older. She could feel time sloughing off her skin with each step, could hear her thoughts peel back in layers as though her mind had to be unwrapped before it could be offered.

She wanted to stop.

She didn't stop.

She told herself she was in control, even as her hands trembled against the wall. Even as her thighs pressed together, slick and aching. Even as the mark on her hip flared to life like it recognized the path beneath her feet.

She should have been afraid.
But all she felt was need.
Wild and wrenching.
Holy.
She had tried to go without him.
And now, she would beg to be taken.
***

Lina felt her soul untether as she ascended the stairs. This was not the cautious climb of a sleepwalker, but the quickening pace of one whose mind was wide awake and gasping. The narrow passage curled around her like an ancient snake, drawing her into its shadowed coil. Air grew tight, pressing down like the thick lid of a coffin. Each step came as a new surrender; each heartbeat pounded with reckless intent. She reached the top and flung open the door, breathless with his name.

Inside, Ezren stood waiting, and though he didn't move a muscle, it felt like his presence filled the room's empty spaces. He was more than just a body framing the doorway; he was a strange and magnetic force, an entity pooling into every shadow and corner. The walls seemed to pulse with the sheer density of him, climbing her skin like smoke and ghosting her senses before she'd even had a chance to breathe. It was as if the room itself had contracted around him, locking in desire and sealing off any chance of escape. Though he was silent and still, his awareness saturated the air between them, a living thing that hummed with vicious purpose. She felt his attention like a physical touch, a whisper of silk that traveled every nerve in her body. When she stepped inside, the entire space beckoned and pulsed, expanding and collapsing in tandem with her own wild heartbeat.

It engulfed her, potent and supernatural. It felt like the start of something she could not come back from.

On her hip, the sigil flared like a heartbeat.

The room unfolded like a whispered secret. Flickering candles cast fragile light across the floor, making the shadows seem more alive than the walls that held them. A tall, dark mirror dominated the far side, soaking in every flicker, every breath, until the air itself appeared trapped within its surface. The mirror drew Lina like an altar, its obsidian reflection half-finished, her own face merging with the shadow. She felt the cold spread of anticipation take root beneath her skin. Her breath came ragged and urgent, the smell of smoke and wax filling her lungs with every inhale.

Ezren stood like an invocation, like a dark god waiting to be worshipped. She had expected him to move, to speak, to give something of himself as she crossed the threshold. Instead, his silence spoke volumes. Her heart slammed against her ribs, a rhythmic plea he hadn't yet granted. She forced herself to swallow, forced herself to fill the chasm of his stillness with her voice.

"You wanted me back," she said. The words hung in the air like a prayer.

"You are the first to ever return on their own." His surprise was laced with darkness, smoke, and gravel.

"And now that I'm here..."

His answer came as a single, ravenous breath: "Undress."

The command echoed, sank its claws into her resolve.

Lina obeyed, a familiar compulsion mixed with something new. She pulled the silk slip over her head, a slow and deliberate unveiling. Ezren's reflection caught her movement, every inch of exposed flesh raising goosebumps beneath the cold air's embrace. She stood in bare skin, in bare breath, the glass fogging before her like an apparition. He stepped behind her, close enough for her to feel the impossible chill radiating from his form.

His breath moved across her shoulders, across her spine, without ever touching—an outline of frost tracing her heat. The flames of the nearest candles bent toward her skin like drawn breath.

The mirror captured their likeness, her own pale frame against the blur of his. She shivered.

"Why won't you touch me?" The question escaped on a tide of need. Vulnerability trembled beneath it, threatening to collapse under its own weight.

He leaned in, each word as intimate and restrained as the exhale that carried it. "Because you haven't begged yet."

The room shattered around her; her knees gave way. She gasped, the sharp intake of breath on an edge she couldn't blunt. Her senses flared in desperation and wonder. Every nerve fired, and Ezren watched her in rapt stillness as she wavered, as she tried to reconcile her body's demands with the cruel distance between them.

Lina wanted to resist, wanted to fight the tendrils of control that curled around her insides and pulled. But they were tangled too tightly, too thickly; they pulled at her resistance, at her defiance, until they were the same fragile thing. She braced herself against the black mirror, and the reflection braced back—cool and wet and trembling beneath her palms, the glass slick from her breath and heat.

And her need. Always her need.

"You're not afraid." It was not a question.

She didn't know, but she realized it was not quite a lie, either.

She opened her mouth, but the words refused to shape themselves. Instead, she closed her eyes and listened: to the pounding in her veins, to the silent spaces between Ezren's words. She opened herself to his unspoken hunger, and when she spoke again, it was no longer a plea, but an offering. "Please..."

His silence became a caress, a second skin she couldn't shed. He watched her reflection, watched as she followed the broken music of her breath, of his proximity. Each inhale became a note, an invocation, spiraling in tempo and tension.

He breathed words into the curve of her shoulder, and they wound their way around her insides until she thought she would come undone.

"I see you, Lina. Do you see you?"

The breath staggered, found its edge. She looked, really looked at her reflection: the flushed skin, the bare contours of herself caught in rapture. Her nipples had hardened, her legs trembled under the weight of wanting. Lina's body shook with effort. She knew this moment—knew it from the dreams she could never fully remember—but awake, in full consciousness, it shattered her. Her belly knotted. Her thighs quivered. Her mouth hung open as she bent toward the desire he wove in the spaces between them, and the ground rushed to meet her.

She didn't remember falling. She remembered his voice, soft and unrelenting.

"You're starting to wake."

She remembered looking at herself and seeing someone else. Her mouth ached, her pulse ached, and somewhere between his first command and her own strangled release, her reflection had smiled.

The glass cleared; the tension didn't. She kneeled in the aftermath, a silent psalm passing between them.

Ezren closed the distance and touched her temple with infinite reverence. The contact was tender and seismic, enough to throw her heart back into disarray. The moment his fingers made contact, the sigil beneath her skin flared—gold, hot, breathtaking.

He didn't look at her directly. He looked only at her reflection, and somehow that gaze was more binding, more intimate. His eyes burned like molten shadows. His lips curled into the barest suggestion of satisfaction. The weight of it was more than she could bear.

When he stepped away, she didn't dare look back.

***

The stairs wound their familiar pattern, each step a testament to something vast and shifting within her. The shadows she had passed through before seemed lighter, less oppressive, but somehow still carrying the heaviness of his presence. Her body felt languid and frayed, a strange and welcome weariness tugging at her limbs. The pulse at her hip matched the drum of her heart, a primal tempo that flared and dimmed beneath her clothes. She paused halfway down, not to rest, but to gather herself before taking the plunge back into what others called the real world.

And the next time she closed her eyes, all she could see was the reflection of herself in the mirror as she offered her passion to a god.

***

Lina felt gravity return the next night at the club, heavy and uncomfortable. It pulled at her in the most ordinary ways: her hair falling limp around her shoulders, the straps of her slip digging into the hollow spaces between bones. She barely noticed the dressing room's usual stench of sweat and cigarettes, barely noticed the noise pounding through the walls. Her own pulse beat louder, more insistently.

Red found her backstage, looking dazed and weightless, and set a skeptical hand on Lina's shoulder.

The touch sent a small, unfamiliar shiver through her body. It felt real. More real than anything else.

The dressing room was a sensory assault. Mirrors at odd angles cut her reflection into fragments. Every flash of her skin against the glass looked foreign and unrecognizable. Each movement seemed delayed, like the world was catching up to the disjointed tempo Ezren had left in her veins. The threadbare couch held the ghost of a sweet incense, struggling beneath the more mundane smells of leather and perfume.

Red's hand stayed on her shoulder, steadying. Lina blinked slowly, coming back into focus. She didn't trust her voice, didn't trust the tremor that she knew would betray the strange delight, the strange dread, bubbling just beneath.

Red was a live wire, pacing in fishnets and combat boots. Her red curls snapped around her face, giving her an electric halo. "You look haunted," she said, the words hanging between accusation and worry. "And high. Like, at the same time."

A breathless laugh burst from Lina's lips, too loud for the cramped space. Her fingers twisted a loose thread at the hem of her slip, raw and fidgety.

"Do I?" she asked, not denying it. She caught sight of her reflection and knew Red was right. The grin on her face felt fevered and too big, a leftover from the mirror.

A leftover from him.

They were a study in contrasts—Red's grounded intensity, Lina's dreamy fracture. The air shimmered with energy. The sigils pulsed beneath her slip, lighting the shadows in rhythmic bursts. Red's gaze flickered to it, dark eyes narrowing with the attention of a wild animal.

She didn't mention it, but Lina saw the way it unsettled her. Saw the way she wanted to understand but couldn't bring herself to ask.

"You okay?" Red asked again, shaking a cigarette loose from its pack and lighting it with a sharp flick of her wrist. The match hissed before the orange glow vanished into smoke.

Lina nodded, though the answer felt like a lie. Like a truth she hadn't fully grasped. "I think," she started, stopping to consider her own thoughts. How foreign and unspeakable they were. How wrapped up in Ezren they had become. "I think I'm in love with something that isn't real."

The admission came in a rush, breathy and astonished, and she almost laughed again at the sound of it. She caught the first real taste of cigarette smoke curling between them, the acrid tang twisting in her lungs. The air seemed to tighten with the weight of Red's silence.

"Ain't that always the way," Red finally replied, her tone bitter and resigned. She exhaled a long plume of smoke, and the frustration in her eyes smoldered brighter than the cigarette.

It was a game they had played before. A dance between reality and delusion, and Lina saw Red's instinct to protect her flaring up like a warning light. But Red didn't understand this version of her. The version whose skin still tingled where Ezren had never touched her, whose breath caught at the sight of her own bare shoulder in the mirror. She felt transformed, but not diminished.

More than she was, and less human all at once.

Her movements felt too smooth. Her voice too soft. Her eyes too wide. There was something languid about her now, something luxuriously slow and stretched, like the aftermath of orgasm or the beginning of a spell.

The sigil glowed fiercely. Its pulse throbbed through Lina's skin, her breath, her scattered thoughts. It marked her and made her. An unanswered question beneath her ribs.

"Lina," Red said, more insistent. The name was both an anchor and a plea. "You look terrible. This isn't a fucking joke."

The words hit like cold water. They cut through the haze, but Lina didn't flinch. Didn't reel back to the comfort of what was real and safe. She touched her fingertips to the warmth beneath her slip and shivered. Not from fear, but from a profound, unsettling thrill.

"I'm not joking," she whispered. Her smile softened, became something closer to wonder. The tension between them snapped, settled into an uneasy truce.

Red saw the certainty in her eyes, the lack of hesitation, and looked away, unwilling or unable to fight against whatever this was.

Lina watched her with curiosity. Watched the way Red flicked ash into the dark corners of the room. The way she refused to give words to the things she didn't understand. It made Lina wonder, made her feel dangerously alive.

They didn't speak as Red turned and left, each footstep like a retreat. The music swelled through the walls, pressing in with bass-heavy insistence. Lina touched the sigil again, its glow casting faint, shifting patterns against the mirrors. Against her reflection.

She sat in the tremulous quiet, dazed and weightless, and the haunted grin crept back across her lips.

THE HUNGER BETWEEN

LINA DRIFTED LIKE SMOKE through the dark alley, knowing he would be there—always knowing. The storm cracked its violent laughter over the sky, and she felt its roar hum through her bones, but she was tired of thunder and of fear. Neon puddles swallowed her reflection, and she felt only the tugging of the hunger inside her, dragging her where she needed to be.

The shadows twisted as they moved toward each other.

"What are you?" she demanded. Her pulse bled against the silence.

"A ghost you won't survive," he said, tasting the air between them, already the wound and the blade.

The storm gnawed at the sky, devouring the stars until only darkness remained. Thunder rattled the bones of the world. Rain soaked the alley, leaving traces of the sky's despair on her skin, but she felt only the flood inside her. Her need pushed against its edges. Each step deepened her awareness, her heart pacing with the finality of finding him. She inhaled the electric night. Her exhale trembled.

Then, finally, she was before him. Waiting like an altar at the alley's end. Unwavering. Unavoidable.

"Ezren." She breathed his name like an answer, a question, a wound. He moved, and the storm screamed as if in terror. He became solid from the shadow, the predator god—always and ever hunger, always and ever the dark temptation.

He didn't answer right away. The air around him shimmered like breath held too long. When he finally spoke, his voice was smoke, and stone, and longing.

"I am what's left after surrender—what survives the letting go."

He stepped closer—silent, unhurried.

"Born in the space between a heartbeat and a moan. Where control breaks. Where need begins." His eyes met hers—red and infinite. "You'd call me Incubane. A thing built to take."

A pause.

"But I never knew what it meant to want until you."

"Why are you here?" she said, drawing nearer, not knowing if she meant the alley or her entire existence. "Why do I feel you like a prayer under my skin?"

Their eyes met, and she saw the night inside him, the pulse of something vast and terrifying. Lightning ignited the sky. Her breath. Her soul. It crashed around them, leaving him silhouetted against the storm. The world seemed to narrow until only he existed. The thunder collapsed against her, the promise and threat of obliteration. He looked at her with eyes that burned like a distant, dying star.

"I'm a hunger," he said, with a reverence that tore at her chest. "A god you woke."

Ezren didn't move—not yet. The shadows clung to his skin like confession. His eyes flickered with restrained violence, but his voice, when it came, was velvet-drenched ruin.

"Because something in you called out—to something I forgot I had." He looked at her then—not like a man looks at a woman, but like a creature looks at a doorway he was never meant to find.

He came closer, like a knife slowly burying itself, and Lina found she couldn't move except toward him. She felt the heat rise between them, saw the familiar crackling glow bloom beneath her skin—like golden veins lit with prophecy. A mark, a bond, the embodiment of her fevered dreams. The sigil bloomed gold beneath her silk slip, branding her chest and hip.

She wanted to hate him for it. She needed not to.

"Because I was shaped to take what others beg not to give. And you…" His throat worked around the words, raw and slow. "You offered it. Soft. Willing. Before either of us knew what it would become." He stepped closer, barely a shift, and yet the air around them changed.

He leaned in, breath cool on her throat. "Because you made room for me—between your ribs, behind your breath, beneath your skin."

A beat. An exhale.

"Is this what you meant?" Her voice sounded ghostlike to her ears. She swallowed, gathered her collapsing strength. "When you said I wouldn't survive you?"

Ezren's eyes darkened—red bleeding into black, like a flame swallowed by its own shadow. But his voice, when it came, was low. Intimate. Unbearably human.

"No." A pause. A breath. "This is what I meant when I said I wouldn't survive you." He reached toward her, fingers hovering inches from her skin—as if even the air between them might ignite. "You were never the one in danger. I was."

His throat tightened like he had to choke the next truth free.

"I meant I would come apart. That I'd starve with you inside me. That I'd break myself trying not to love what was never meant to be mine." And then—barely audible: "I didn't know you'd still choose to touch me, anyway."

"What if I don't care?"

His mouth curved like an answer. His silence made the night throb. The thunder roared again, swallowing her fear. "You're more than I thought," he said, and his voice crashed over her like the storm.

Lina bit down on a scream. The breath left her lungs.

"And still less than you want," she said. The accusation turned in her heart, bleeding truth and desperation.

His smile was darkness and salvation. He became more, filling the space between them with the terrible beauty of his nature, as if he couldn't hold his shape in the weight of what he felt. For her. A god. A ghost. A need.

Her legs ached with the urge to run—to him, from him, it didn't matter, so long as she was moving. But she stood, suspended on the wire of her will.

"I don't understand how to want you," she said. It came out as a cry. "When I can't have you."

"You already do." His words cut into her.

She closed her eyes. Saw him like a bruise against her closed lids, still there, even when she tried not to look. She felt a shiver from the center of her.

He let her drown in the silence before the storm's collapse. "You are the first thing I've ever wanted to crave me."

She gasped. Let the air flood into her until she shook with it. Her heart filled the spaces between them.

"Then take it. Take me." She pushed her voice through her need.

A touch of disbelief broke his gravity. He pulled it back, drew the storm into him, and gathered himself. Her courage made him tremble.

"What am I if you stop?" Her voice pulled him closer. Her voice collapsed the distance. Her voice bled and ached with everything they were.

"Alive." The word burned like an offering. He crossed the last of the space until his cold brushed her skin.

Her fear spun into desire, flickered bright and searing. His breath froze against her neck, and she wanted its ice, she wanted its blaze. The storm tore at the sky again, shook it loose, and she caught her breath. Lightning crashed and burst above them, reflected in a thousand puddles, flashing around them like a broken star.

Lina reached for him. She rose and caught his mouth with hers, before she lost the last of her will.

Her lips opened, soft and furious. She fed him the violence of her hunger. Her mouth on his was consuming, brutal, sacred.

It shredded reality, sent the storm screaming.

His restraint trembled, as thin as paper, as breakable as silence. He stood to take, to claim, to break. He was the moment before the fracture, the glint of the blade. But he let her unravel him, let her smash the floodgates, let her break against his reserve like waves. The world tilted, burst, and drowned around them. His arms closed around her as if it were he who needed protection. The charge was more than electricity, more than nature or will.

Her marks burned under her skin, gold, and alive, and brilliant.

"Ezren." His name tumbled from her as the night lit with her fire. As the dark bent and twisted. As the storm crashed, and they with it.

She came apart with the sound of the sky's collapse. Her release was violent and primal. It was more than her body and more than her mind. It was more than she was, and more than she knew how to contain.

Lina broke the kiss, collapsed against him, shuddered, and cried with everything she was and wanted.

His heart bled the silence.

She felt his need, raw and untamed, held tight inside his chest.

His breath escaped in shards. "I didn't feed. I didn't take." He struggled, trembling against the loss of himself. "You gave."

The air stilled, unbearably dense and torturously quiet. Lina clung to him as if she feared gravity, feared breathing, feared anything that meant space between them. She burned with her own gift. The charge was oppressively thick. It should have been everything she feared.

The lights in the alley flared, flashed, flickered, and broke. A drop of water hit the ground with the weight of a hundred thunders. Her own ragged breath deafened her.

His shoulders shook.

And still she clung, afraid of nothing but distance.

"If I stay," Ezren whispered, his voice breaking against her temple, "I'll destroy you."

And then he was gone.

***

Lina slipped through time like a drowning girl, gasping for air and pulling back nothing but breathless minutes.

Days without Ezren grew teeth. She survived on insomnia and desire. She left her meals like tiny sacrifices, offering up uneaten bits of self.

At Nocturne, the stage became her escape from the pain that his absence had wrought in her guts. But her audience turned savage with her unraveling demanding that she give even more.

Lina pounded on Ezren's door to throw herself at his mercy. But he didn't answer.

Three days since the alley, but each day dragged like a starving creature, fierce and insatiable. Lina's world crumbled into one long stretch of absence, hungering for his touch, his presence. She drank her coffee like it was liquid need, taking it in heavy gulps until her hands shook and her eyes glazed over. Her reflection in the bathroom mirror was gaunt and unfamiliar. It stared back at her with shadows like bruises and lips bitten raw.

Four days since the kiss.

She curled up in bed, but sleep betrayed her. She wrapped herself in her sheets, in his scent, in the weight of everything they were and couldn't be. His words played in her mind like broken records, endlessly turning. They bruised the air, and she held her breath until her chest burned.

You are the first thing I've ever wanted to crave me.

Lina shut her eyes against the world. But the world kept watching.

On the fifth day, she slipped into Nocturne and let the door close like a breath behind her. The crowd surged like a living thing, tangled in its own heat and flesh. It screamed with a pulse that matched her own. She ignored the mirrors, ignored how the walls seemed to bend with her movement, how the lights chased her. They felt like haunted eyes, but she didn't care. All she needed was the stage.

Lina stepped into the light, and the music became her body. The world fell away, left her and the rhythm alone to feed. She danced, spinning, drowning, catching breath only to lose it again. Her feet were raw against the wooden boards. She ached in every place she should have touched him. Her eyes closed to the world. The crowd swallowed her whole, and she shuddered, felt the bright energy crackle beneath her skin. Her own breath rose like a storm as it pulled her apart.

Someone yelled from below. "You're not dancing. You're disappearing."

Her breath shattered. She came back to herself like waking from a nightmare. Her legs were jelly. Her heart wouldn't stop.

She stumbled offstage and into the dressing room, alone with the heavy night and the even heavier want. She dropped into a chair and held her chest, her lungs desperate and hollow. The mark was bright against her skin, molten, and alive, and wanting.

"Girl, what's gotten into you?" The voice came out of nowhere, sharp and hard, as it pulled Lina from her mind.

Lina looked up, trying to remember how to speak. "I don't know." Her words fell out.

"Is it drugs?" The girl, Red everyone but Lina called her, narrowed her eyes. They were suspicious, full of glassy hurt. "Is it some man? Because whatever he is—he's not normal. Mick says it feels like something's haunting the place. Like a curse or something."

Lina hesitated, then whispered, "I'm fine."

But even she didn't believe it.

Cassie bit her lip, watched her a moment longer, and said quietly, "You don't look well, Lina. You look possessed." Then she turned and left.

Lina's hands were still on her chest. Still empty. Still shaking.

***

At the bar, Mick poured a drink with hands as steady as mountains. He didn't need to look to see.

"Has it started?" he asked. His voice didn't rise above the hum of the club—it just was, like the foundation beneath their feet.

Lina blinked. "Has what started?"

He set the glass down and wiped the rim with a clean cloth, like the question had dust on it. "The thing that takes people like you and doesn't let go."

Lina felt herself sway, felt the room sway with her. The night caught her like a lover.

"Is that why he's gone?" Her voice cracked the words. She needed them answered. She needed them spoken.

Mick gave a slow shrug, more weariness than indifference. "Maybe. Or maybe he's waiting to see if you're the first one who walks out whole."

He didn't offer comfort. Didn't explain. Just watched the way her eyes darkened like he'd seen it before. Because he had.

She left him with his bottles and the bass. Left him like they all did. But this time, he didn't look away.

***

Lina walked the crowded streets until they were empty. Her need was louder than any other noise, louder than all the bodies in the world. She found the bed she couldn't sleep in and let her thoughts collide until the pieces were small enough to inhale.

Ezren came to her that night, at last.

In her dream, he was fury and salvation. He filled her mind and her body until she couldn't tell which was which. His touch cut through the world. Her skin sang. She woke drenched, exhausted, more alive than waking allowed.

He was the silence, and he was the storm.

She tried to hold him in her dreams and her bed.

She was never enough.

Lina found the stage again the next day. She let it eat her, let the music bleed and rise until she forgot how to move without its promise. Her body was electric, born of its need and his. Her breath became the crowd's, harsh and holy. Her hands tore at her skin, at the binding desire.

She fell and let herself unravel. It was Cassie who found her this time, Cassie with hands too small to save.

Lina slept, and he filled her.

Lina woke, and he wasn't there.

Time stretched, breaking at its edges.

Her pulse filled the cracks.

***

Lina climbed the stairs that night with nothing left but the weight of him. His voice haunted the hollow between her ribs. His absence was a bruise pressed to every breath. Her thighs trembled with memory, her lips parted with want. Still, she moved. Still, she rose.

She counted the steps like she was counting heartbeats, each one a vow: He's there. He's there. He has to be there.

At the top, she paused, her fist hovering. The closed door pulsed in time with her fear. She knocked—once, soft, sacred. The wood sighed beneath her touch like a lover catching breath.

Her heart made no sound.

Then the door opened.

Ezren stood in the glow of candlelight, shirtless, trembling, the deep ridges of his ribs hollowed out like carved ruin. His eyes were rimmed in red, fevered and raw. They dragged over her—cheeks flushed, dress clinging to sweat-slick skin, pupils blown wide with ache. Her nipples peaked through lace. Her legs were bare, already parted in surrender.

"You're breaking," he rasped. His voice was gravel and thunder and something older. "I can feel you falling."

She stepped inside without a word, placed her hand on his chest. He was ice and need. Her palm curled over his heart like a brand.

"Then break me," she said, and the plea wasn't soft. It was a command dressed in white silk.

Ezren flinched. Closed his eyes. His silence answered, and it wrecked her.

When he opened them again, his irises were fire and ruin.

"This is the last time," he warned, even as his mouth lowered to her throat.

Lina arched, her head falling back to bare the curve of her neck. "Good."

He kissed her there—not gentle. His lips seared the skin just above her pulse, and when his teeth grazed down, she gasped. He pushed her against the wall, pressed her there with his entire body. She felt the length of him—hard, desperate, shaking—through the thin press of fabric. Her thighs clenched around him, and he groaned into her neck.

His hands dragged her dress up, up, until it bunched around her hips. He dropped to his knees like worship, hooked her legs over his shoulders, and pulled her open.

His tongue touched her—hot, inhuman, reverent.

She screamed.

It wasn't slow. It wasn't sweet. He devoured her like he had tasted nothing in centuries. Like she was the only thing that had ever fed him.

Lina writhed, fingers knotted in his hair, pulling him deeper, grinding against his mouth. Her cries echoed through the stairwell, into the shadows, into the storm that had never stopped breaking above them.

When he rose again, her thighs were wet and shaking. He didn't lift her—he pinned her. His body caught hers as she wrapped herself around him, both arms, both legs, like he was the only solid thing left in a world made of smoke.

He pressed into her in one long, devastating stroke.

She broke.

She shattered around him. Her back bowed. Her head hit the wall. Her nails dug crescents into his shoulders. Her moan was an offering and a threat. She clenched around him so tightly he gasped, faltered.

He buried his face in her neck.

"Anymore," he said, broken, panting, pulsing inside her, "and I'll destroy you."

"Then do it," she cried. "I want to feel the end. I want it to be you."

His pace faltered. Then surged. Then lost itself.

He fucked her like confession. Like punishment. Like prayer.

She convulsed with the second orgasm before the first even faded, her screams swallowed by his mouth. The sigils on their bodies pulsed gold, then white, then something darker—something sacred.

She sank to the floor as he pulled out, her body limp and spent, slick with sweat, blood, pleasure.

A wreck.

A shrine.

Ezren stared at her like she was the last true thing in the world. His breath sawed through the quiet. His hands reached for her—but didn't land.

He couldn't touch her. Couldn't bear to. Not now. Not when it meant everything.

He left her there, fading into the dark smoke of the mirrors. Her name left his lips like broken glass.

She used the shards to cut herself free.

WHAT'S LEFT BEHIND

LINA WOKE ON THE bathroom floor of the Nocturne Lounge.

When her eyes opened, she felt unstitched from herself, lost in a landscape of scattered mirrors and daylight so bright it flayed her senses. The tile was cold against her cheek, her limbs tangled beneath her like discarded threads. Her skin stuck to the floor in places—damp, raw, aching. Her fingers twitched. Her breath came in hiccups. Her mouth tasted like salt and something hollow.

She lay there, sprawled across the Nocturne's cold floor, amidst jagged reflections that sliced through the heavy quiet. Her thighs bore dark, flaked reminders of something she couldn't name, and though she pressed her fingers against the sticky traces of blood, she felt nothing. Silence suffocated her. The entire world was stripped bare and sterile.

Red was crouched over her, not speaking, not moving, just watching with wide, dark eyes rimmed in smudged liner. Her hand hovered inches from Lina's shoulder, like touching her might break something sacred—or something dangerous.

"You're scaring the fuck out of me," Red whispered. Her voice cracked like glass.

But Lina couldn't grasp the words, couldn't reach out or return the warmth that Red pressed against her in trembling arms. It was like being deep underwater, hearing only the muffled echo of her own longing.

"What the hell, Lina?" Red's voice finally broke through, edged with fear. But Lina had nothing to give back.

"I don't know who I am without him," she whispered, knowing that even those words no longer felt like hers.

Lina tried to sit up. Her body refused. Her stomach heaved once, dry and useless.

The mirror above the sink had fractured. Jagged cracks spread outward in a spiderweb from the center, and in the shattered reflection, Lina saw herself in pieces—mouth open, lashes wet, skin gray. Her sigil pulsed faintly beneath the torn edge of her slip, flickering like a dying star.

Her hand shook when she lifted it from the stickiness on her skin. The crusted blood fell like old ash, almost colorless, insignificant. She lay there as though she might sink through the tile and disappear entirely. Light pushed in through the half-boarded windows, turning the nocturnal space unfamiliar and vast. Even the mirrors that once bent reality were ordinary now—cracked glass instead of portals to the unknown. Her pale limbs sprawled unnaturally in the empty air, and her skin had none of its earlier flush. Bruises bloomed where his touch used to spark fire. She brought her knees up to her chest, shivering in the stark light. She thought about getting up, but couldn't imagine why it mattered.

The chill from the floor seeped into her, a slow invasion. She wrapped her arms around her legs, closed her eyes, willed herself to remember warmth. Nothing came. No pulse, no breath, no sense of the hunger that had driven her. Only blank spaces where Ezren had filled her—mind, body, soul—and a dull ache of something broken, a mirror splitting itself down the center. She blinked, watched a spider-web crack etch through her vision, and realized it was happening inside her head, not in the room.

Without him, she was nowhere.

No one.

She forgot about Red until her friend's hands grabbed her shoulders, shaking her back to the surface.

Lina opened her eyes again. Red kneeled, cherry curls spilling forward, fierce eyes searching for something recognizable in Lina's vacant expression.

"You look like hell," Red said, her voice breaking. "What happened to you?"

The words ran together, distorted and distant. Lina tried to reply, but it was as if she had forgotten how to speak. Her mouth opened, closed, formed no sounds that meant anything. Instead, she looked at Red with eyes that felt alien, part of someone else's body. Someone without heat or breath. Someone whose limbs weighed nothing, whose heart did not beat. The silence between them swelled until it was louder than the unsaid words.

Lina heard herself from a distance, faint and without conviction: "He's gone."

Red squeezed her shoulders tighter, as though pressure might bring Lina back from whatever void she had slipped into. "No shit. You're acting like you're possessed or something, Lina. Jesus. You have to get it together."

Lina touched her lips. They were cold. The absence of him, the absence of everything, froze her from the inside out. The cold tile beneath her no longer registered.

Red's arms cinched around her like a lifeline, but the sensation felt like it belonged to someone else.

"Say something, Lina," Red demanded, voice a fragile mix of irritation and fear.

Lina watched her own pale fingers touch the place where a sigil once glowed. It was gone now, like a ghost finally exorcised.

"I don't know who I am without him," she said again, more to herself than to Red.

Red's embrace tightened, an angry insistence. She wrapped Lina in her own jacket, pulling it from her shoulders with forceful hands.

The black denim swallowed Lina's naked frame, the sleeves hanging well past her fingertips.

Red smelled of sweat and cheap perfume and anger.

It should have overwhelmed Lina's senses.

It didn't. Nothing did.

"I knew this would happen. I fucking knew it," Red whispered, more breath than voice, like she was afraid the shadows might hear. "I've seen it before—the way this place chews through girls like you. The lights change. The mirrors lie. And something old starts watching you from the cracks in the floor." Her arms tightened, but it was like holding smoke. Her warmth barely touched the cold. "I told Mick. I told him it was starting again."

Red pulled Lina closer, whispering into her hair like a secret. "We need to get you out before it finishes what it started."

Lina let herself be lifted, limp and untethered. The lights overhead were too bright, but she couldn't bring herself to blink against them. Even her reflexes had deserted her. She watched Red's mouth move, saying things she couldn't follow, couldn't absorb, couldn't answer. Then it was only the echo of her own last, fraying tether: "I don't know who I am."

They didn't speak again until Red helped her to the car, silent except for Lina's shivering breaths and the slow drip of rain off the gutters.

***

Lina didn't remember falling asleep.

But the emptiness when she woke was sharp and immediate.

The sheets were cold. Damp. The mark at her hip was only a shadow now—duller than she'd ever seen it. Her hand skimmed over the spot and found no answering heat, no pulse of gold beneath the skin. Her body felt quiet in a way it hadn't for weeks.

Too quiet.

She lay still in the bed that had once held his scent and stared at the ceiling. Breath shallow. Eyes wide. The ache lived deep, like something lodged between her ribs. Not sharp—just constant. Just there. Like a wound with no blood. Like the ghost of an orgasm that refused to fade.

The mirror across the room remained blank.

Its surface reflected only what it should—her body curled into itself, her skin pale beneath the thin gray light leaking through the window. She waited, long enough to forget time, for it to shimmer, for a flicker, a breath, a ripple. But it stayed still.

Indifferent.

Dead.

She reached for the sigil again. Still nothing. Her breath caught in her throat.

She wasn't used to silence anymore. She wasn't used to this much gravity.

The apartment felt stripped bare, as if every sensual thread had been pulled loose. No music. No scent of wax or smoke. The shadows didn't cling. The light didn't bend. Her skin didn't tremble.

Her hunger was still there, but it was directionless now. Unfed and untouchable.

Lina sat up slowly, knees to chest, arms wrapping around herself. The sheets fell around her like forgotten lovers. Her nipples peaked from the cold. She didn't shiver. She didn't feel enough to.

For a long time, she did nothing but breathe.

And then she whispered his name. Just once.

Nothing happened.

Her throat tightened.

She rose, naked and aching, and walked to the mirror. She stood in front of it—watching herself breathe, watching the faint flush in her cheeks, the bruising around her thighs that hadn't yet faded. She lifted her hands, ran them slowly across her chest, down her belly, between her legs. Her fingers slid through slickness that didn't surprise her. Her body still remembered what it wanted.

But it wasn't enough. There was no answer. No tremor in the glass. No breath but her own.

She turned away before the tears came.

The kitchen was no warmer. The light had gone flat.

She made coffee and left it untouched. It sat cooling beside her like a ritual without meaning. She couldn't remember the last time she ate something that tasted like anything. Her body felt like a thing worn thin. Her hunger had nowhere to go.

She wanted to scream. She didn't.

Instead, she dressed in silence.

Not the silk and white lace she wore for him.

A hoodie. Jeans. Bare feet on cold floor.

And then she stared at the door.

And then she opened it.

The city outside was loud, wet, indifferent. People moved like they didn't notice the storm that had broken something sacred inside her. She passed faces and caught none of their eyes. She might have been a ghost. Or a girl hollowed out by her own wanting.

Nocturne rose before her like a memory. The doors were open. The lights were dim. Music bled through the walls.

She didn't go in. She couldn't.

She just stood there, barefoot and unsteady, and waited for something to call her back.

Nothing did.

So she turned.

And walked away.

***

The music still played, but the beat that had pulsed beneath their skin like a second heart felt muted now, flat and unfamiliar. With Lina gone, Nocturne's lights flickered without pattern or promise. It was as if she'd pulled every current of heat and desire with her. Even the air was thick and colorless, stripped of any hint of what she'd once been and what she'd made them feel.

They still came—drifters, seekers, those drawn to the edges of something unnameable—but she wasn't there. Not on the stage, not behind the shadows. Their eyes searched the dim corners, waiting for the flicker of her ghost, and when it didn't appear, they slunk away unsatisfied.

The quiet thickened night by night, wrapping the club in a weight that settled in the lungs like grief. It was her absence made tangible—dense, breathless, and cruel.

Mick lit a cigarette and watched the dancers fill Lina's empty space. He exhaled smoke and regret, then walked the corridors, closing up.

It was late.

Or early.

The hours folded into themselves, all meaning lost in the stretch of time between when she had last danced and now. Her reflection still haunted him, her memory more tangible than the empty rooms and hollow stage. Her ghost lived in the mirrors. He was sure of it, more certain than anything else he'd seen vanish into the night. Her name hung in the air like smoke, curling into places she used to be, then disappearing.

"Lina!" he called. His voice echoed, more like a memory than a sound.

The stage lights cast his shadow along the walls, black against the movement of the mirrors that did not show him the answers he wanted. He'd seen her—he was sure of it. He'd felt her—more of her than anyone else had left behind in this place. He flicked ash and tried to breathe in her absence, tried to see the patterns where they used to be.

Nothing. Only echoes and ghosts.

He heard Red's steps behind him, quick and anxious. He didn't have to turn to know what her eyes were asking. She'd been doing the same for days now. She hadn't seen Lina since she'd found her curled and unresponsive on the bathroom floor. They were all looking. All of them. Even the ones who'd left thinking there was nothing else to see.

He touched Red's shoulder, let her hear the unsaid weight.

"I thought I saw her," he said finally, letting go of the rest of the words.

She looked at him, both hopeful and incredulous, knowing how much he kept to himself.

"Or maybe it was just the memory of her," he added.

His voice was hoarse from more than just smoke.

"The mirrors?"

"The mirrors," he confirmed.

"And now?"

He shrugged. A thousand thoughts in that slight gesture. "Maybe we lost her. Like the others."

Red refused to let that be the end. "If she's still out there," she said, fierce and sure, "I'm bringing her back."

"Some people don't want to be found."

"You're wrong," she shot back, louder than he'd heard her speak in days. Her boots echoed along the empty hallway as she stormed away. "I'm not losing her."

He watched her go. The space around him swallowed her footsteps, but he knew she would be back. Girls like Red always came back—fighting, scarred, but still standing.

The ones like Lina?

They didn't belong to the club.

They changed it.

And when they left ... it never stopped echoing.

"I'm not losing her," Red's words rang in his mind.

But the mirrors still held Lina's ghost.

The floorboards creaked beneath Mick's weight as he locked up, echoing with the same familiar uncertainty. She had made them all feel more than they'd known. Now she left them to unfurl, to hollow themselves in her absence.

He dragged deep, the smoke clinging to his lungs like regret, then exhaled slow—like a man who'd done this before, and already knew how it ended.

***

The knock at her door came in the late afternoon. Lina had been sitting on the kitchen floor, knees drawn to her chest, head tipped back against the cabinet, staring at nothing.

She didn't move right away. The sound felt too far, too soft, like it belonged in someone else's life. But the knock came again—firmer this time, followed by the creak of a familiar voice.

"Lina. Open up. I brought soup and judgment."

Lina pulled herself to standing. Her legs tingled, half-asleep. She crossed the floor at a snail's pace, every step an act of will. When she opened the door, Red was standing there with a plastic takeout bag in one hand and a cigarette tucked behind her ear.

"You look like shit," Red said, brushing past her.

"I feel worse."

"You're not dead," Red said. "I was starting to take bets."

Lina didn't speak. She stepped aside. Red walked in, tossed her keys on the counter.

The door shut behind them. Lina stayed by it, arms folded tight across her chest, like she wasn't sure she wanted to be seen.

Red set the bag down on the counter and lit the cigarette with a click. "You haven't come to the club. You haven't answered your phone. I half expected to find you curled up like a dead thing with candle wax on the floor and Latin scrawled across the walls."

"No candles," Lina said. "No Latin."

Red squinted at her. "Just death-vibes then. Good to know."

The silence filled in the spaces between their words, heavy and breathing. Red took a drag and exhaled slowly, watching Lina like she might shatter under the weight of eye contact.

"You look worse than when I found you on the floor."

Lina nodded. "Feels worse."

"Mick said the Lounge feels haunted," she said. "The regulars keep looking for something in the shadows. They think it's you."

"I'm here."

"Not really."

"I'm not eating," Lina said.

"You're going to try." Red's voice softened. "Have you ever considered something? What if this isn't love? What if it is something else?"

Lina turned to her; eyes wide and calm in the worst possible way. "Does it matter?"

The air stilled. Red didn't answer.

Instead, she pulled two bowls from the cabinet and poured the soup, moving like ritual. "You're going to eat something. You're going to drink some water. And then you're going to tell me what the hell happened."

Lina didn't argue. She sat down and took the bowl with both hands, fingers trembling just enough to spill. She stared into it like the broth might answer her. Held the spoon. Didn't lift it.

"You're falling apart," Red said. "Whatever he is, whatever this was—it's not just in your head anymore. It's effecting you physically."

"It's not in my body anymore, either."

Red stepped closer. "What does that mean?"

"He's gone," she said finally. "It means I can't feel anything. Not like I did. Not when he was..." She swallowed. "Touching me. Being in me. Around me. And I think I broke whatever was between us."

Red's spoon paused mid-air. "Broke it how?"

"He said it would be the last time, so I severed it. Cut whatever force tied me to him. I thought it was the only way to breathe again. But now..."

"Now you can't breathe at all."

Lina nodded. Her breath hitched.

The soup cooled in her hands. She didn't take a bite. Lina sat.

The cigarette burned low. Red flicked the ash into the sink. "Jesus, Lina. Why?"

Lina stared into the bowl, watching steam curl like ghosts. "Because I couldn't breathe. Because I was lost. Because I thought if I cut the thread, I'd find my way back to myself."

Red didn't speak. Just let the silence stretch. Then she leaned in, elbows on the table, eyes narrowed beneath the flicker of overhead light. "But how did you even let it start? What was it about him?"

Lina's eyes lifted. She looked at Red, but not really. More through her. Past her. "He was the only person who ever made me feel anything."

Red blinked. "What kind of thing?"

"Everything," Lina whispered. "It was all gray-scale before him—like I'd been underwater my whole life and didn't know it. Then he touched me, and suddenly I couldn't stop drowning in color. Fire. Hunger. Breath I didn't know I had."

Red leaned back, cigarette between her fingers. "And that scared you more than being numb?"

Lina nodded. "It wasn't love. It was obliteration. I couldn't find myself in it. I couldn't tell where I ended, and he began. Then he said it was the last time. It was too much. And I wanted it to stop."

"So you severed it."

"I thought if I tore it out, maybe I'd go back to before. To the quiet. To the cold. Anything but that aching, unfulfilled need."

"And did you?"

Lina's silence was the only answer.

Red leaned back like the realization physically shifted something in her. "Jesus, Lina ... you're in love with him."

Lina didn't flinch.

"This isn't a possession," Red said, more to herself than Lina. "It's love. Real. Messy. Dangerous love."

Lina turned to the window and whispered, "I know," and the words felt heavier than grief.

***

While the club felt stripped and numb, Lina's apartment felt like a mausoleum, devoid of everything except memory and the aching hunger for more. She moved like a ghost through the colorless rooms, silent, hollow. The fabric of her old white slip floated around her thin form, the place of her vanishing almost unrecognizable without its usual chaos and sensuality. Cold, abandoned, and forgotten. Like the rooms themselves were disintegrating in protest of the choices she had made. She heard only her own breath, shallow and unsatisfying. Not the heated pants she remembered, just the pathetic, defeated whisper of half-life.

The echo of what she'd had reverberated against the walls, flickering images of a self she could no longer find.

She missed him. Missed him inside her. Missed herself inside of him. She missed the unspeakable becoming hers and wanted more than anything to give in.

"Ezren," she had said, before she'd let herself believe it was possible to sever, to survive without him.

But now there was only the unbearable hollowness, and she knew she couldn't.

She stopped in front of the full-length mirror, stared at the reflected ghost of her own body.

Paler, gaunter, unfamiliar.

The sigil had faded, barely there, and her skin had lost the glow of being known, wanted, taken.

She touched it. She felt the absence, the shameful blankness of surrender's aftermath.

It wasn't just a mirror that looked back at her; it was the lost and forgotten memory of the connection she had broken.

The realization cut through her, cold and cruel.

She let the thin slip fall to the floor. Her body was bare, but nothing about it felt exposed. She had known his touch, had memorized its texture and heat, and now it was only memory, an afterimage of things she couldn't reclaim. She'd tried to forget it, to forget him, but her own flesh was a reminder that would not release her.

"Ezren," she had whispered. "Ezren." But now the name had no meaning, no heat. No claim to what she had chosen to un-feel.

The defeat was exquisite and brutal.

She placed her palm against the glass, closed her eyes, and waited for the pulse, the promise, the illusion that used to spark to life beneath her fingertips.

Silence stretched.

Cold, indifferent silence.

Nothing happened.

Her reflection did not bleed and blend like it once had. Her breath left no mark, no fog on the glass. The mirror's chill was a lover who had forgotten her name.

"Ezren," she whispered, her voice cracking on the name like ice on a thawing lake.

The mirror splintered from corner to corner, its shards falling like unkept promises.

It echoed through her apartment, through her body, through everything that used to be her.

It echoed and echoed and echoed.

***

That night, Lina tried to take herself apart.

She locked the door, turned out the lights, and lay on top of the covers with her legs spread and her eyes open. One hand drifted down between her thighs. The other rested on her stomach, trembling with every breath. She didn't close her eyes. She didn't pretend.

She needed it to be real. To be hers.

She moved slow, mapping her body like a stranger's. Her skin was sensitive, tight, aching beneath her own fingers. She traced the lines he had followed. She pressed into the places that once sparked beneath his breath.

But nothing opened. Nothing cracked.

Her body remembered how it used to respond—how quickly she'd climbed for him, how easily she'd burned.

But now it was all friction. All effort. Her pleasure hovered behind a locked door.

She wanted to scream. She didn't.

Her fingers moved faster. Her chest rose in sharp, shallow gulps. She begged herself to feel it. She tried to recall the weight of his voice, the chill of his breath, the sear of his restraint.

But nothing came.

Only sweat. Only breath. Only the hollow beat of disappointment.

When she came—if it could be called that—it felt like a cough. A stutter. A mechanical flicker of nerves with no soul behind it.

She wiped her hand on the sheet and curled onto her side.

And cried.

Not from pain. Not from want.

From absence.

***

Sleep came late, dragging her under like a tide that had waited long enough. When it did, it came heavy and strange.

She found herself back in Ezren's room, but it wasn't the same. The candles were unlit. The mirrors dulled. The air was too still.

He stood across the room, shirtless, barefoot, silent. His obsidian horns—once veined with glowing sigils—were dull, the markings faded like forgotten runes. His black wings hung limp behind him, heavy and slack, their edges curled inward as if mourning. He looked carved from shadow and ruin, hollowed out by everything she had taken with her.

His eyes were dark and rimmed in red. Not glowing. Not cold. Just tired. He looked thinner. Less. Faded. Hollow. Like a shadow of himself trying not to collapse.

"You severed it," he said. "You are the only one who has done so."

Lina wrapped her arms around herself, as if that could hold her together. "I had to."

He didn't move. Didn't breathe. Just watched her, his presence heavier than any storm.

"You're drowning without me," he said.

She didn't argue. She couldn't deny it.

"I know."

The mirrors behind him pulsed once. A dull shimmer. Like something inside her trying to wake.

Ezren took a step forward, then stopped. "I should leave you like this. Let you come through it alone. It will hurt. But you'll survive after a time." His eyes flashed with a brief anger. "I should let you sink."

"But you won't," she whispered.

He looked at her then—not the way he had before, not like a predator or a god.

But like something lost.

"I won't," he said.

Lina stepped closer. Her hands trembled. "I don't want the absence anymore."

Ezren didn't touch her. His eyes burned, soft and dark as his voice folded into her like a promise.

"Then come."

TAKE ME

LINA PROWLED THROUGH THE city's slick streets like a ghost—a saint—a goddess, and its dark, breathless night. She left nothing in her wake. No blood-red footprints on the sidewalk. No shadows cast against the brick walls. Not even an echo of the night's heat. Only a single frayed thread fluttering behind her, like a warning. By the time it caught the night's desperate grasp, she had already entered the closed Nocturne Lounge through a rusted side door.

The club's emotional pulse encircled her in waves—warm, then cold, then warm again. The walls breathed. The floorboards quivered beneath her weightless steps. No bass or heartbeat broke the air, only silence stretching longer, deeper, more wrong with each stride. She moved as if she could control its distortion by sheer will. Her bare feet on the floorboards. Her eyes on the spiraling staircase that ascended beyond this world. Her sigils beneath her skin. And her mind on Ezren, starving and her own need.

The hallway narrowed, then widened, and then narrowed again. Like a noose. Or a lover's arms. Lina's blonde hair hung loose around her like the starlight of the night, tendrils clinging to her skin and whispering against her back as she glided forward. As she approached the stairs, their metal skeleton creaked in protest, bending slightly beneath the weight of its own shadows. She placed one foot, then another on the first step, smiling as she ascended, thinking of Ezren and how he would receive her gift.

Would he resist? Would he fade away entirely? Or would he break beneath the force of her new desire?

Each step drew her closer, and the narrow staircase seemed to hold its breath. The wooden rail was cold against her hand. She wrapped her fingers around it as though taking a lover by the wrist, squeezing tight, knowing that soon enough Ezren would be beneath her again—breathless and supplicant—writhing under her control. Her footfalls struck in time with the wild rhythm of her pulse, and her mouth was slightly open, lips parted as she ascended to meet her altar.

The door to Ezren's chamber stood open, revealing him like a prayer. The hallway stretched its last, and she paused there at its ending, regarding him with eyes that burned and flickered like the soft, shifting candlelight that bled out from the room and into the dark.

Ezren crouched on the floor, and shadows fled his emaciated form like smoke from a dying fire. They pooled around him and stretched long tendrils that twitched along the floor. That reached, pleading, toward Lina. And trembled as she let them touch her, a faint golden halo that defied them. The room was everything—blood, breath, light, reflection—at once, and the creature who was its center, who was its god, was more raw need than he was substance. He held his head in his hands, his once powerful body starved and trembling, barely held together by desperation and want.

She took a step toward him, moving like a supplicant toward a dying altar—her eyes tracing the hollow plane of his chest, the way his ribs jutted like bone-wings beneath bloodless skin. His obsidian horns had dulled to matte ash, and the sigils carved along them flickered dimly, like prayers half-forgotten. His wings—those once-monstrous, leathered things—hung limp behind him, dragging against the floor like remnants of a fallen god.

Her energy pushed into the room ahead of her.

"You're dying," she whispered, half command, half confession.

His head rose. His eyes found hers.

Black, they were. Hollow and old as midnight. Hollow, but not empty. A fevered light circled the darkness there, dim and fading and full of unanswered hunger.

"I refused to feed," Ezren said, voice hoarse and breaking. "There are others, but none of them taste like you." His eyes lifted to hers, hollow with ache. "What I take from them turns to ash on my tongue. Yours..." He faltered, as if saying it cost him breath. "Yours is the only surrender, the only offering I crave."

The words fractured as they left him, barely more than breath and ache. Then silence, thick and trembling.

He did not move. Only a tremor passed through his frame—like need trying to rise through broken ribs. Around him, the candles guttered. His hunger pulsed through the room in rhythm with the low, flickering light.

And Lina felt it.

Felt the fire still burning in him—small, but stubborn. A flame that remembered her skin, her voice, her blood.

A fire that would only rise for her.

She took another step, an even slower one, feeling the weight of her control and knowing how heavy it would fall on him. She took that step and a million more, all in that one simple motion. And then she let her coat fall around her ankles.

Naked, glowing, marked as his—his—and more than his.

A goddess. Marked with glowing runes of life. A wound and a gift.

Lina arched her spine and stood luminous before him.

"You don't get to die," she declared. "Not until I say you can."

Ezren did not respond, not at first. Not with his mouth or his voice. But his eyes widened, bleeding fire and red like blood through every shadow that trembled and shrank in the room. And his body—ravaged, half-starved—flickered in time with hers, pulling desperately at the energy that burned beneath her skin, igniting a raw and terrible beauty.

With shaking limbs, he rose on his knees to meet her. His joints cracked like dry tinder that lay before a raging flame. His limbs cracked, but not his composure. Not yet. And when he spoke, his words did not break. "Do you know what you are offering?"

Lina glided toward him, slow as hunger, her mouth a wound that hadn't healed. The heat of her body hit his like a storm front—sweat-slicked skin, pulse thrumming with gold.

"You," she said, voice like velvet dragged over a blade. "Your breath, your blood, your fire—I want it writhing beneath me."

She leaned in close, the heat of her thighs brushing his.

"You're mine now, Ezren. Not to break. To burn."

Then pushing him back on his heels, she straddled his lap with intention. Sacred, sure, in control. Her warmth sparked through his fragile frame like wildfire, and for the first time in ages, he found himself hungry for something other than essence. He hungered for her blood.

Ezren groaned, and his hands moved to her hips. But they trembled and pulled back again, and when he met her gaze this time, his eyes bled black. "No," he said. "You'll break."

He had meant the words to be a command; but they fell weak, like prayer.

"You'll starve," she answered, a faint smile pulling at the raw edges of her mouth.

This time, Ezren's fingers found her thighs, and he felt the living pulse of power that surged through them. That bled into him. And from the force of that energy, from the depth of her own intention, he felt the rhythm of her heartbeat. Felt it merge with his. Felt her strength—unbroken—become his own.

***

His broken groan shattered against her lips, echoed in her mouth. She swallowed it whole—let it fill her lungs like smoke, like sin—then gave it back to him with a guttural moan that vibrated through her chest. Her mouth dragged over his, open, hungry, claiming. She sucked the sound from his throat and bit down, soft flesh and sharp teeth, until he gasped her name like a wound that bled devotion.

"Lina."

She drank it in—his groan, his need, his voice—a trinity of longing that lit up her spine. And then she moved. She shifted her hips, angled her thighs, and sank down onto him with a wet, exquisite slide that stole both their breaths.

He filled her slowly, thick and trembling, his length twitching inside her like he could barely contain it. She was drenched and ready, her heat clenching around him in greedy pulses, as if her body had already chosen him in the dark before her mind ever caught up.

"Stop," he begged, the word ripped from his throat. His head dropped against her shoulder, mouth at her neck, breath hot and shaking. "I can't control it. I'll destroy you."

She bit his lower lip, dragged her tongue along the seam of his mouth, and ground her hips down until he cried out again.

"No," she said, voice molten, sacred. "You'll complete me."

Then she moved—slow at first, deliberate and devastating. Her hips circled, then rocked forward, guiding him deeper inside her until she gasped from the fullness. Flesh met flesh in a slick, greedy kiss, her body accepting every inch like it had been carved for this alone. She bore down on him with raw intention, grinding, milking, riding the edge of sensation like it was her altar.

Ezren arched, his spine snapping taut, a fractured breath breaking in his throat as she rolled her hips again and again. His hollowed frame convulsed beneath her, muscles seizing with each stroke. The storm inside him—hunger, fire, need—erupted and lashed out, clawing at her through the bond that had never truly broken.

But she didn't shatter. She rode the wave. She opened wider. Took more. Demanded more.

His claws dug into her thighs, bruising, reverent, anchoring himself to the one thing keeping him from spiraling into nothingness. Her. Lina. His. The only tether he had to reality, and the only reality that ever mattered.

"Lina," he rasped again, the word guttural, holy, as if her name alone kept him from being unmade.

And then he thrust—hard, uncontrolled, feral—his hips slamming up into her with a force that bordered on savage. The sound of their bodies meeting was obscene, slick, beautiful. He fucked her like a starved thing, like a god unraveling at the feet of his worshipper.

But she was no supplicant.

She was the storm.

She bore down harder, gasping through her own pleasure, through the bloom of climax building at the base of her spine. She knew the rhythm of his desire better than he did. She met every thrust, every trembling growl with a slow, merciless grind.

"You're mine," she breathed, teeth grazing his throat. "Not a god. Not a ghost. Mine."

Ezren trembled beneath her, monstrous in form, but undone. The edges of his form flickered—sigils glowing, horns humming, jaw trembling with restraint.

"I'm not yours to consume," she whispered against his lips, her voice a blade of silk. She clenched around him and dragged a scream from his throat. "I'm yours to worship."

And he did.

He worshipped her with his body. With his surrender. With every trembling, unholy moan torn from his throat as she rode him like he was made for it.

Because he was.

Her sigils ignited, streaking across her skin in lashes of living gold—marking her not as conquered, but as consecrated. Every line shimmered like scripture, holy and profane, a gospel of pleasure burned into flesh. The glow spilled across Ezren, branding him in turn. Her ribs lit his chest. Her spine claimed his back. She blazed her name into his soul with every thrust, every gasp, until the light became unbearable.

They weren't moving anymore. They were being moved—by the force of something ancient and erotic, something made only for this union. Light bled from her, as if her body could no longer contain the enormity of what they were.

And when his need crested—when he could no longer hold the god inside him—she bit down. Hard. Her lip tore. Blood pooled on her tongue, given to him in her kiss.

But it wasn't enough.

She dragged a nail across the curve of her chest, split skin, and opened the altar. Her blood flowed—warm, wet, divine. She smeared it down her breasts, across her throat, over the trembling swell of her belly. A consecration. A command.

Ezren snapped.

His grip bruised. Anchored. Reverent and ruthless all at once. He buried his face in the blood-wet valley between her breasts and roared. Not like a man, not even like a monster—but like a worshipper breaking under the weight of devotion.

His mouth found the wound. His teeth pierced. Her blood spilled into him, thick and sacred and full of power. He fed—and it wrecked him.

He convulsed. Jerked.

His back arched so hard he nearly bucked her off, but she stayed atop him, thighs locked around his hips, hands gripping his horns. She rode the violence of his surrender, let it rock through her until their screams overlapped and shattered the quiet between worlds.

And through it all—she did not falter.

Because this time, it didn't break her.

This time, it broke him.

His body seized under her, spasming, overloaded by what she gave and what he took. His climax surged through him like a ritual undone—raw, blinding, eternal. He came undone in her arms, and she caught him as he fell.

They screamed each other's names like incantations, summoning power, summoning truth. And the mirrors exploded—not in ruin, but in revelation. Their joined reflection fractured into dozens of burning fragments, all showing the same thing: union.

Surrender. Divinity made flesh.

He was hers.

She was his.

And when it was over, the stillness was sacred.

Ezren clutched her like she was the last warmth he'd ever know. His skin slick with sweat, with her blood, with the radiant pulse of shared magic. She held him, her body still trembling, the sigils now pulsing in tandem across both of them—not as warning, but as rhythm.

Not hunger. Not frenzy.

Balance.

***

He held her close, his frame lean and trembling against the radiant thrum of hers. His arms, once forged for control and conquest, now curled around her with reverence, with awe. His lips brushed her shoulder—light, broken, worshipful. And when he spoke, his voice was the low thunder of aftermath, the brittle crack of something long-frozen finally breaking open.

"Lina," he breathed. "You've made me want to be more."

Her response was flame and breath, threaded with the certainty of one who had already burned and risen. Each syllable etched into the air with quiet command.

"You already are."

Ezren drew her tighter still, until there was no space left between their bodies. Her skin was heat incarnate, radiant with purpose. His was shadow—cool, scorched, starved—and where they touched, the dark did not dim the light. It bent to it.

His breath stuttered. She could feel it—how he trembled, how his soul flinched in awe of her. She lay draped against him, and he let her. Let her claim. Let her quiet the trembling ache in his limbs, now heavy with something he'd never allowed himself to hold.

And in that stillness, something moved inside him. A strange warmth uncoiled through his chest, across his obsidian-marked arms, down the ridged length of his spine, threading through the sigils that once bound him in hunger and command. It slid over his antlers like candlelight, seeped into the tattoos that had once been warnings. Now, they were promises. Now, they glowed not from power—but from peace.

He didn't understand it.

But she did.

Lina pulled her coat around them like sanctification, tucked her body tighter against him, and moved with the grace of a storm gone gentle. Her breath ghosted along his neck, warm and honeyed with jasmine, a scent of softness born from fire.

And when she spoke again—soft, slow, dark with owner-ship—it wasn't a question.

It was a truth made flesh.

"You're mine now."

Ezren's eyes closed. And for the first time in his eternal, aching existence —

He wept.

Not from weakness. But from release.

From having something he'd never dared to want.

From belonging.

The room pulsed around them like the space between heart-beats—thick with aftermath, with devotion, with the holy ruin of who they had been. The air itself held them like a spell, heavy with salt and sweat and the copper of shared blood.

Together, their bodies entwined, their essences braided tight, they watched the glow of their sigils soften—no longer blazing with hunger or need.

Now, they pulsed like a vow.

Dim gold and deep red.

Thunder after rain.

Jasmine and blood.

Heat and surrender.

Sanctified.

THE DOOR IN THE DARK

THEY HAD BEEN LOST in the seething darkness, bodies folding into one another like shadows consumed in fire, her pulse a war drum against his ice.

The locked room held them tight, binding them within its collapsing frame, as though it, too, strained under the force of their reunion. Light fractured and spilled across the ceiling, tumbling across the walls like broken moons.

He gathered her to him, let his monstrous need swell inside him—threatening to undo them both. Yet this time, he held.

Lina's power charged the air between them like a lightning storm.

Her mouth opened in a soundless wail as he took her again—searing, complete.

It erupted and pulled at her—not to shatter, but to forge. She rose through it, molten, whole.

She was everywhere. In his eyes. In his blood. In his hunger.

And then, for the first time in his ageless existence, he felt something unnameable take root, transforming him as they soared to their ecstatic climax. Every last thread of his darkness detonated into the night, a silver burst of energy that smashed through the fragile barriers of their reality. Everything shattered, releasing all it had contained in an explosion of glittering light and sound.

Lina drew her breath back in from the silence that followed, claiming it. She floated in the surreal aftermath, feeling his tears spill onto her throat and cool the fire in her skin. She felt the world settle, felt

Ezren still inside her, felt his sobs fill the air with something both pure and desperate.

His ancient pride was gone, discarded, nothing more than scattered shards on the floor. Her power had eclipsed his, and instead of cursing the darkness, he kneeled in awe of it.

Lina's hand touched the softness of his hair, ran along the arch of his horns, coaxing his face to hers. They hung in the moment, suspended in a new truth that trembled like the silvered edges of broken glass.

When she kissed him, it was gentle and long and said everything she had no words for. When she finally stood, it was with deliberate grace, with limbs that trembled but did not falter.

Ezren watched as she slipped from his embrace, her body pulsing with the energy that his once-mighty form could no longer command. He remained kneeling, witness to her raw, resplendent beauty.

The sigil above her heart glowed in time with her breaths, gold, then not; like the knowing eye of an ancient god. Blood streaked down her legs, a river of evidence that merged with sweat and shone like holy water.

He saw her clearly. He saw what she had become, what he had helped her to be, and what he would never again control.

With a reverence he had never believed himself capable of, he lowered his gaze to the floor.

"I love you," he whispered to her, retreating, as if it had always been a truth he'd feared to name.

Lina paused. Her bare foot brushed across the shattered glass, uncut. Her entire frame seemed to lift, to hover in the unbroken space. And then she moved away, trailing her scent, and warmth, and silence, like a prayer behind her.

Ezren's voice followed her. His old pain slipped from her skin like oil.

The heavy door creaked as she opened it, releasing her from more than just the room. As she stepped into the hallway, everything around her shifted, and she welcomed it with unblinking eyes.

Walls shimmered with an electric hum. Time warped in eddies around her. The world bent to her will. The Nocturne Lounge became a vessel of new creation, teeming with life where only ghosts had lingered before. Her spirit walked the corridors as though newly born, like a dark goddess named by her own breath.

In the moments before she pushed through into the human world, Lina glanced over her shoulder one last time. Ezren remained hunched on the floor. Glowing fragments encircled him like stars held captive in shadow.

The things she had feared most now belonged to her. The things that had owned her were now owned in turn. He had given her this. He had wanted to give her more.

"I honestly love you, too." She smiled, a faint flicker, then turned away, leaving the echoes of what was in the expanding space.

She stepped outside, out of shadow, out of time, into a world remade by desire.

And even here, she still heard him: a soft, reverent murmur rising from the hollow shell of what he'd once been.

It filled the space between her heartbeats, not hunger—but becoming.

"Because of you ... I exist beyond hunger."

***

She was gone for weeks and everywhere at once.

Her energy stretched and filled the building, remaking it, naming it with her breath. Nocturne's new life thrummed inside its walls, a velvet heartbeat that drew the curious and the lost to its cavernous depths. They came, hypnotized by the sigils reflected in Lina's eyes, magnetized by a space that shimmered with an erotic pulse. Her body moved like smoke, drawing even those who never dreamed of following her.

Her whisper settled over them: "Come in. Let me take you."

Light glowed from the open doorway like an opium dream, gold and warm, curling into the cool night, calling out to them. Bodies lined the street, tight with hunger, and lust, and awe, waiting for a glimpse of something they couldn't yet name. Inside, shadows slipped across walls, snaked over floors, coiled around limbs, twining flesh, and longing, and air, until they were indistinguishable from one another.

Her absence had made the club into something holy, and the congregation grew with each passing hour.

The soft flutter of fabric sounded through the space like wings. Candles flickered, wax tears spilling onto the floor like ghosts. Breathless voices carried from every corner, repeating her name, her power, her transformation in hushed, fevered tones.

"I heard she came back," someone whispered near the bar.

"Heard she was reborn," another voice murmured through a silvered reflection.

"Heard the dark became hers," came the half-dreamed echo from the other side of the room, from beneath the tangle of bodies in a booth, from beneath the tangle of limbs on the dance floor.

The space pulsed. It writhed. It sighed. Blood-red lace swathed the club, cascading from the rafters, shivering like the hem of a ceremonial garment.

A throb of music vibrated the walls, rhythmic, desperate, consuming. It rose from beneath their feet like a beckoning tide, flooding the room with heat and urgency. They closed their eyes, lips, fingers around each other, every motion building into the next, and still it would not stop.

Still the music moved through them, rose through them, drew them together and into itself until they became one with its burning breath.

Her breath. Her magic. Her sanctuary.

Lina was the new religion, and she moved among them like a prophet. They were hers, and she let them worship in flesh, in desire, in prayer that consumed them more wholly than anything they'd ever known. She let them drown and rebirth themselves in the sea of want.

She let them touch and tremble and believe.

She walked through the crowd in soft, white lace, eyes like glowing embers, marks on her body alive with power.

She no longer performed. She took. She received.

Voices hushed when she passed, bodies parted to let her through. The light that seeped from her skin caressed each soul she encountered, claiming them, making them her own.

Some reached out to her, trembling hands that never quite met their mark. Others just watched, wide-eyed and rapt, afraid to even breathe the same air she did.

Her body swayed like smoke, but she was no longer the girl who carried the weight of unshed dreams. Now, she was the one who gave them, shaped them, let them live inside her until they burned like stars.

She walked pas a grasping, entwined couple against the wall, hips joined in holy supplication. Her mouth curved into the briefest of smiles, and they both gasped as they drew in the sharp breath of climactic creation. Another girl, young, fell to her knees in Lina's path. She touched the girl's bowed head, and the fragile creature shuddered, gasped, and held on tight to the slender wrist of a woman who, just moments before, had been a stranger. Her unspoken prayers took form, and she, too, was transformed.

Ezren lingered in the edges of Lina's sight, as constant and steady as the light she gave. He watched her without hunger, no longer driven by a need that devoured him, but by a love that sustained.

Lina met his gaze and felt their new balance settle across the space. They were two, and they were one, and this time it was forever. He gave a slight nod and stepped into shadow, his body a sinuous breath of presence and absence. As he turned, the faint shimmer of a sigil glowed briefly at the center of his back—no longer devouring, no longer burning.

It pulsed once in time with hers, then dimmed like a candle fulfilled.

She closed her eyes for the barest of moments, basking in the energy that spilled from every surface, spilled from him, from her, from the legacy of what they'd built. When she opened them again, they blazed brighter than before.

They blazed like memory, like salvation, like a promise she never doubted would be kept.

She was about to speak when the murmur of a crowd made itself known. They gathered, expectant, waiting for him, for her, for themselves.

Lina let her whisper ripple through them, never stopping, never satisfied, never needing to: "Come in. Let me take you."

The crowd surged forward, bodies entwined and fluid, a sea of ink, and skin, and lust, and silk. Each had heard the call, and each had answered.

Her call.

Her answer.

She watched the movement rise and fall, a tidal rush of exquisite longing, and she knew this was exactly how it should be.

Exactly as she was.

Red stood on the stage like she had never danced before. She had taken her name to heart and draped herself in its vibrant folds. Every scrap of fabric, every shard of lipstick, every stroke of eyeliner was an offering, and she flung them to the eager hands of her acolytes, abandoning herself to the hungry air.

Lina saw her eyes alight with wild flame, saw the arch of her neck as she let herself be taken. She was once a body on the edge, unsure, struggling, caught. She was now a question in motion, free, whole, burning to know how it would all end.

Red threw her head back, lips parted, and whispered to the crowd—

"This is the kind of fire you don't come back from."

Mick ran the bar with an ease that only decades of knowing too much could bring. His glass-filled hands never wavered, but Lina caught the upward curve of his mouth as he watched Red's new form take shape. He had tried to guard them all, to save them from becoming.

Now, he poured the drinks, understanding that some fates were simply meant to be.

She moved away from them, the sigil on her back painting the dark with gold.

Her footsteps carried her to the front of the lounge, where her next follower waited outside the door—wide-eyed, trembling, afraid but ready to step inside the fire that had remade her.

Her next offering. Her mirror. Her first loyal follower in this new beginning.

The girl was slight, fragile, brown hair wet against her skin, her teeth digging into an uncertain lip.

She was ink on a white page, a raw body in a world not yet defined.

She was Lina.

And she was not.

Lina stood like a flame on the other side of the door from the younger woman, radiant and waiting.

The other's shy, outstretched hand toward the door reflected in her knowing eyes.

She watched through the Flemish glass in the door, as the girl turned, not yet brave enough to meet the brilliant sun in her path.

She remembered the girl she used to be—the one who flinched at the light, but opened to darkness.

The dark door was a question, an answer, a crossroads where life began anew.

Lina reached and opened the door, luminous and confident; opening the way first.

Her voice cut clean through the shadows, through the light, through the breath, and flesh, and the building itself.

"Come in. Let me take you."

The girl turned back, hesitation a second skin that she would soon shed.

Lina held her smile, held her hand, held everything the girl would soon offer, everything she would reclaim.

They stepped across the threshold entering the world of the Nocturne Lounge together: reborn, re-birthed, revived.

Finis

Somewhere, another door waits in the dark—
another girl, another monster, another prayer about to be answered.

THANK YOU FOR READING!

Did You Enjoy This Book?

Please tell your friends and don't forget to leave a review on **Amazon and Goodreads!**
Reviews and ratings like yours are the life's blood for independent writers and small publishers!

Want to see more by V. P. Nightshade?
Visit her Author Page on Amazon
   https://www.amazon.com/author/vpnightshade

www.ingramcontent.com/pod-product-compliance
Lightning Source LLC
Chambersburg PA
CBHW051313170626
46809CB00004B/1877